The Possibility of eRada

Leslie Thomas Flowers

Copyright © 2024

The Possibility of eRada by Leslie Thomas Flowers

All rights reserved. No part of this book may be reproduced in whole or part, or stored in a retrieval system, or transmitted in any form or by any means, electronic, mechanical, photocopying, recording, or otherwise, without the written permission of the author.

ISBN 9798335929530

Dedication

This book is dedicated to my children, their father, and my grandchildren … and to you and yours, as well.
Never stop dreaming about a better life for us all and know that what you dream will come true if you aspire to be in lockstep with our creator.

Acknowledgments

Birthing this book took the expert guidance of Frank Zaccari and Melissa van Oss from Trust the Process Book Marketing.

To Dennis Pitocco of BizCatalyst 360° who provided a platform to write and publish this story from the outlined developed twenty-five years before.

To video producer, creator and imagineer Aaron Gibson for the seven-minute book trailer, depicting my vision of eRada, as though it was his own.

To Paulette Hallam and Nicole Angai-Galindo for walking with me every step of the way, keeping me steady and focused.

To Sylvain Ruest, for providing the inspiration and context for this story, some twenty-five years ago.

And to all those who lifted me up and brought this baby into the world to share.

Thank you one and all.

Leslie Flowers

Foreword

The Possibility of eRada

A Spellbinding Tale Where Fantasy and Reality Intertwine

Every so often I come across a rare book such as this that draws you in so quickly that you simply can't put it down. In this mind-bending novel, Leslie takes readers on an utterly unique journey that blurs the line between reality and fantasy. Inspired by a young woman's incredible story seemingly too vivid to be pure fiction, this book will leave you questioning the very nature of what is possible.

Some years ago, the author crossed paths with the mysterious woman who would become the muse for this genre-defying tale. She spun a narrative so intricate and alive with detail yet seeming too fantastical to be true. Unable to dispel the story from her imagination, Leslie has cleverly brought the young woman's account to life in book form, titled after the magical realm at the center of the drama.

Seamlessly bridging contemporary adventures with high-fantasy worldbuilding, "The Possibility of eRada" is simply unclassifiable within standard genres. Leslie's masterful prose brings even the most imaginative details to tactile life, immersing readers in the hypnotic and convoluted cosmology of eRada. This is no traditional hero's journey, but rather an out-of-body experience that lingers long after the final page.

Whether you view this parable as imaginative fiction or a transcribed true account from an extraordinary source, the book is undeniably an exquisite literary achievement. As all great fantasies do, it probes the boundless extents of human imagination while revealing deeper insights about the fabric of existence itself. An unforgettable tour de force, this sweeping odyssey is simply a must-read for anyone who has dared to dream of what other worlds may exist across the inner dimensions of reality.

All things considered –this novel is profound storytelling at its very best.

Dennis J. Pitocco
Publisher & Editor-in-Chief
BizCatalyst 360°

Introduction

Right around 2000, driving back and forth every weekend for months, four hours each way along Interstate 40, straight across North Carolina, I became bored. The road is long and straight, and I could keep cruise control 'on' at 60mph nearly the whole way.

I was in deep pain; my three-decade marriage had dissolved, poof! without my agreement, and I was lost. Really lost. The family roots built with the love of my life, were broken. Kids were on their own and I was walking on earthquake rubble, hoping always to keep myself balanced. It seemed impossible.

I covered my pain by falling in love. That love was how I kept my mind off my woes, when it all became too much. Was it real? It was as real as my then seventeen-year-old emotional self could love.

During those four-hour drives, I began to play with my imagination by visualizing scenarios and places that appealed to me, and the hours flew by.

Maybe it was like lucid dreaming, dreaming awake, as cruise control was doing its job. I was feeling great as each week I visually crafted another scene using my creative imagination. And time flew by.

I arrived in the mountains each Friday (I made a rash decision to open a chocolate company in a small cabin in the mountains, knowing nothing about business or chocolate ... but I didn't care).

When I pulled up the mountain road and climbed the stairs to the cabin, the first thing I did was document what I had visualized during each four-hour journey there, on my computer.

The characters, a new place to live, how eRada was formed, who managed eRada, who were the inhabitants, the climate, topography; how it became inhabited.

It was all made up ... to pass the time and revel in the wonderful memories of that incredible feeling of love in a place where everything felt right.

I had no interest in writing the story. Right then I was busy helping my partner make (and sample) lots of chocolate truffles.

What I know today is why I didn't write it then, and why I couldn't.

I've learned that the universe, my cocreation partner in manifestation, preferred to not provide the end results until I was ready…I had finally learned enough in two decades by matching the vibration of the size of this story so that I could not only write the story … I could enjoy the whole process of birthing it.

I had no clue that this playing with visualization held my true soul; and that this idea of eRada was or could be big. It was a way to pass the time after all.

Once you read The Possibility of eRada, you may wish to match the story progression with the twenty-five visual elements found in the seven-minute trailer found here on *YouTube*.

This book is for me the perfect melding of living a life of values, virtues, and soul-kissing love. Please join me.

Table of Contents

PROLOGUE	1
ONE	5
TWO	9
THREE	13
FOUR	17
FIVE	21
SIX	25
SEVEN	31
EIGHT	39
NINE	45
TEN	51
ELEVEN	55
TWELVE	61
ABOUT THE AUTHOR	65
INSIGHTS AND DISCOVERIES	67
CREDITS	94

PROLOGUE

When she arrived at the nursery that day after work, she didn't see him anywhere.

She quickly walked around the plants and shrubs and then hurried to the small business office in the back.

The owner of the nursery was running numbers on an old adding machine when she walked in. It jammed after pressing almost every key, so he stopped every few seconds, adjusted the keys, grumbled, and continued, repeating the pattern.

He was engrossed in this task so he didn't hear her come in, over the tapping and straightening the machine keys.

She watched for a minute or two and then interrupted, "excuse me, sir" she said as he looked up at her. "I'm looking for Van. Do you know where he is?"

The man looked at her, paused and then stood up, stretching his legs, then lifting his arms above his head, cracking his knuckles. Then he asked, "Come again? Who?"

"Van!! The student intern working here from the university!." she said, trying not to sound too irritated because he took so long to answer her to begin with, and that she only had a few minutes left to catch the bus. "He's studying agriculture there."

"There's no Van working here," the owner said and turned back around, sat down and began running numbers again.

Before he got to the third key, which stalled, she asked, exasperated by now, "you mean he did work here and now he's gone?"

The owner slowly turned back around, looked at her, paused and said, without getting up this time, "Look, I don't know what you are talking about young lady. I have never had an intern here from the university and the only helper I have is my granddaughter when she is on break from school, and she's sixteen."

"But that's just not possible," she thought she said to herself, but likely not to say it out loud, as he shook his head, went back to work, as she hurriedly walked out of the office, back through the nursery, having one more good look for him, and out of the shop and on to the bus stop.

As she ran bleary-eyed now to the sidewalk outside the nursery, the fragrance of the cedar trees hit her in the face and literally stopped her in her tracks. She sneezed, and then ran all the way to the bus stop.

Lee cried on the ride home … that's her name, by the way … Lee.

Her tears were heavy and salty, and she wasn't even sure why she was crying. She thought … I'm melting like the disc. She had been rolling it around between her fingers in her pocket again as she heard the bus bells and felt each stop and start along the way home.

Lee fell asleep that night, tears on her pillow, asking out loud, "Van, where did you go? Were you even there? Were you a dream? Am I crazy … because I know I felt your arms around me."

Leslie Thomas Flowers

ONE

Some years ago, I met the girl in this story. She wove a tale so life-like and yet what seemed so impossible, I decided, with her permission, to write about it. It all started about sixty years ago near the 'City by the Bay;' San Francisco.

Episode One — the Beginning

It was a fitful night for the girl. Heavy, salty winds from the rain over the Pacific pummeled the trees outside her bedroom window, inside a colorful, cozy room in a third-floor turret of an unkempt Victorian.

The house stood on three acres of woods, across the Golden Gate Bridge in Marin County, and was now owned by the girl's mother. It was rumored it once belonged privately to the famous San Francisco madam in the 1940s, Sally Stanford, who ran her business in 'the City' and kept this for her 'special' customers. No one really knows the true story.

The storm whipped the trees against the windows in her room for hours and she awoke at sunrise, groggy and tired the next morning. The sun was shining, though, so she hopped up, threw on an old Pendleton shirt and jeans, and took her normal walk by the small, wooded stream on the property to her mother's cottage, about five hundred yards off the dilapidated back porch. Down four steps she went to catch the path as she did every day during the week before work, to have a cup of coffee, and a talk with her mother.

It was spring now and the short path, lined on both sides with newly crowded blooming purple crocus beds. The girl walked quickly, kicking to the side any one of a number of branches left on the path by the storm. They lived in what she always thought was an enchanted wood, where the Dogwoods her great grandfather carried from North Carolina to plant near their new home, some seventy-five years ago, bloomed every spring. When she squinted her eyes and looked into the woods now, the white Dogwood petals looked like a dusting of light snow, always in mid-fall. Continuing on the path, she kicked something that flashed for a second, further down the path, along with a bit of debris.

The thing caught the light again and the girl reached down to pick it up and have a look. It was clear, smooth, iridescent, and oval, about two inches long, one inch wide, and half an inch thick. It was hard and cool to the touch, like glass. As she turned the disc over and over in her hand, her hand became damp, then wet. The disc was melting like Ice! "But how?" she thought, wiping her hand on her shirt. It felt cold in her hand. In one second, the girl squeezed her nostrils together with her fingers (like she inhaled pepper) and when she did, she quickly took an involuntary, sharp breath in through her nose, and saw, what she remembers as 'seeing stars,' and then coughed twice.

She pulled out a crumpled tissue from her pocket, wrapped up the disc and put it in her vest pocket to examine again later. It was such an odd object ... it certainly wasn't natural ... it looked like a fake cabochon the girl used to buy from the craft store when she was in her jewelry-making days some years ago.

She arrived at her mother's. As she stepped up onto her mother's small wood porch, as she did every day, she stopped short. The flower boxes! Her mother had a green thumb the boxes were overflowing as usual with assorted colorful blooms. They almost seemed to glow; like a light was shining on them ... and from within them. The girl didn't remember them looking this way yesterday or any other day she told me. She was sure. And she knocked.

She forgot about the disc in her pocket, had coffee with her mother, and took the path home to get ready for work. She got into her work clothes, which included a hand-me-down Villager shirtwaist dress and a large apron which covered her dress completely. She hung her Pendleton with the disc in the pocket on the chair and didn't think about it again. The girl worked in a candy shop in San Francisco and was learning to make chocolate truffles under the guidance of a seasoned master.

There is more to the story.

Tune in for Episode Two ...

The Narrator asks:

What was that disc?
Why did it melt?
What were its properties?

TWO

After a long day's work in the candy shop in San Francisco, where the girl was learning to make truffles, she continued telling me her story over a coffee when we met at the café next door. That night she arrived home after the daily bus ride across the bridge and made a beeline to her bed. She thought she smelled the ocean as she began drifting off … yet felt no accompanying breeze on her face. She was unusually tired tonight and was ready for a good, long sleep

Episode Two — Origins

She was dreaming now, in deep slumber.

She saw from somewhere high in the heavens above earth, something odd, yet somehow familiar.

Lights were flashing through the sky in various places at different times, and at odd intervals.

Looking down from above, she thought she saw the makings of a game … it looked like a baseball game! It was! A sort of baseball game!

There were twelve players, and they were the twelve astrological constellations. They were immense, each covering miles and miles across the sky!

BAM! Taurus batted a sphere with lighted projectiles and began moving his great expanse across the sky.

As the image of the sphere with points expanded to fill her full field of vision, it looked like a little sun.

A 'sunvirate' she thought. as it was again batted, this time by Capricorn.

In her dream she tracked the sunvirate through the heavens, and then it disappeared. The lights were no longer visible. It was gone.

A lucid dreamer, she easily followed the tracks in the sky by moving her vantage point across the heavens, far above the game, by slightly leaning in the direction she wanted to go.

The movement was gentle like the controls of a large aircraft. A 'slight lean' and she glided to another vantage point of the game. Lean the other way, and slowly she glided back across the sky.

Capricorn hot-footed it across the heavens to stop at a small bright cluster of stars.

Aries was next up to bat. A new sunvirate appeared and the game went on.

Now dawn was breaking, and the girl began to awaken to start another day. Feet on the floor, the dream slowly disappeared from her thoughts and was quickly replaced by getting ready for work.

Tune in for Episode Three …

The Narrator asks:

Where did that sunvirate go?
Why is it important to this story?
Still wondering about the glass disc from episode one? It's coming!

THREE

The girl awoke the next morning to the sound of thunder. Her dream slipped away as her thoughts turned to getting ready for work. She was learning to temper chocolate this week. Tempering causes the crystals to be small and consistent to create the best, smoothest and most tasty chocolate. The shoppe ordered only the best product from Belgium, along with organic flower essences. Each truffle was rolled by hand and the girl was learning that technique too.

Another long day, when she got home, she hopped in the shower.

She forgot to bring her robe into the bathroom, so she grabbed the nearest thing to put on … the Pendleton was close by, hanging on the same chair since she left it there since the day she found the glass disc.

She loved Pendletons. These were her dad's; he had given her his prized collection of six. They were wool and a little itchy, yet so warm and colorful. They smelled like her dad too; always comforting.

They were also perfect for the weather when worn as a jacket. When it got warm in the afternoons, she tied the arms of the shirt around her waist. Worked perfectly for the cool, foggy mornings that turned into sunny afternoons particularly during 'Indian Summer' in the fall. That was the warmest time in the City.

She felt something in the shirt pocket. Oh! It was that odd disc she found on the way to her mother's. She took it out of the pocket and realized it got wet the moment she touched it. In the next second she squeezed her nostrils together with the fingers on her right hand (like when she inhaled pepper) and when she did, she quickly took an involuntary, sharp breath in through her nose, and saw, what she remembers as 'seeing stars,' and then coughed twice. She had a light dinner which tasted extra good and went to bed.

Working chocolate took a lot of energy.

Episode Three — Finding eRada

She was dreaming again, in a deep, warm and soft slumber in her turret.

She was right back to tracking where that sunvirate had gone. It disappeared and while the game continued among the immense astrological signs, lumbering around the heavens, unaware of their size, with a new ball, the girl focused on its landing point.

She saw it! She saw sparkles intermittently from quite a distance. As she 'leaned' across the sky to get closer to it, it had lodged in an odd, elliptical shaped planet. Damaged, it sparkled only now and then.

The Possibility of eRada

At first glance, the tiny planet had two suns and in what seemed an instant, as if by magic, the sunvirate loosened, shot upward, and took its place as the third sun of the planet!

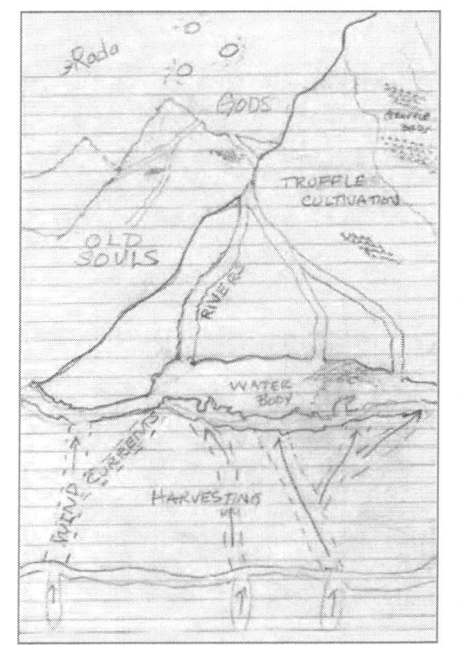

Unfortunately, the damage disallowed this sun to rotate with the other two; it remained constant in the sky.

The dance of the two rotating suns, anchored by a constant one, created climate and day and night on the planet "eRada," she mumbled, and she turned over, punched her pillow down, buried her head deeper, and drifted away again.

As the girl continued telling me her story, when we met her during her break at the chocolate shoppe. And I drew this map of eRada on the back of a brown paper bag that held stacks of napkins together when they came back from the cleaners. I worked quickly as she explained all the features on this odd, shaped planet. I was fascinated.

I worked quickly as she explained all the features present on this odd, shaped planet. I was fascinated.

She started with the three suns at the top and how one of them was the sunvirate from the game she watched the night before.

She explained to me how the sunvirate became the third sun maintaining day, night, and climate. How would that work, I wondered as she talked away, lost in the exquisite description she was sharing with me.

Her break was over, and she invited me the next day to continue telling me more.

The Narrator:

Now you know the *sunvirate* became the third sun, giving 'life' to this odd-shaped planet.

When the disc shows up again, its purpose will be revealed soon.

In Episode 4, I learned all about the unique climate and topography on eRada, amazing on its own.

FOUR

I couldn't wait to hear more about eRada. We made plans for the next day to meet again on her break.

The girl walked through town every day after work to catch her bus that took her across the bridge. She passed the bookstore, the hardware store, and then the nursery on the corner. These small shoppes where a comfort as they were the ones that were there since the 1950's with some embellishments and upkeep. It was cozy. It was comforting; a great way to wind down her day and get lost in her thoughts.

Just now, though, her thoughts were interrupted as she passed the nursery ... a bronze flash of light in the dusk caught her eye ... coming from somewhere amidst plants and shrubs. Still walking she turned her head to look back into the nursery.

When she saw it again, she stopped, turned toward the light, and stepped into the front of the nursery. In the back, behind a cluster of shrubs, she saw the light flicker again. It was the quick glint of a floodlight in the dusk, bouncing off the shoulder length, coppery hair of a tall, slim young man working there. He looked up.

She turned and walked toward him smiling. She had never seen him before yet was somehow compelled to approach and to speak to him.

His name was Van, he told her, and had started that day as an intern for the nursery as he was working on a degree in agriculture at the local university. He laughed a moment ... then reached over to wipe off a glob of dried chocolate on her sleeve. "Tell me you work at the chocolate shoppe," he said smiling. She shook her head 'yes.'

Episode Four — Climate

With thoughts of how she met her new friend Van on her mind coupled with another particularly exhausting day, it was only moments after a quick bite to eat that the girl flopped onto her bed in her turreted alcove and fell into a deep sleep.

As she dreamed again of eRada, she was able to maneuver herself far above, and all around the planet, which was quite beautiful. The temperature was steady at 65°F; no change (not so different than San Francisco she thought inside her dream).

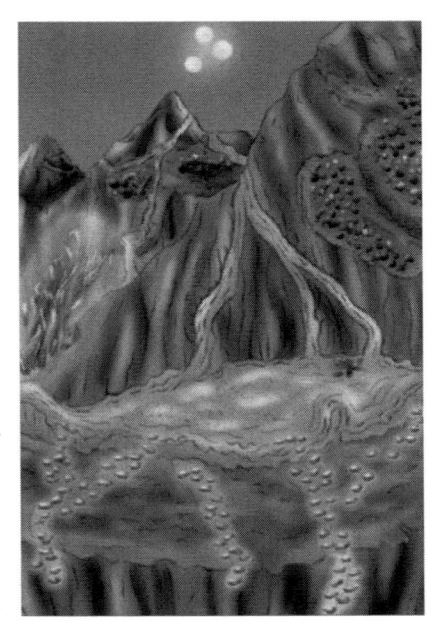

The odd shape allowed only four hours of night for each twenty-four and with the constant sun and temperature, glorious wild truffles erupted naturally through all the moss beds in the mountains. Each truffle was infused with and exemplifying one unique virtue.

The truffles were cultivated and harvested by the population along the mountainsides in the upper elevations of eRada. They were then packaged for shipment within eRada, far below the planet surface.

At the closing of each day, a basket of eRada's wild truffles was offered by the people to the 'Beloved One,' with thanks for the gift of life in this beautiful place and their daily labor of love. The offering took place in the small village square near the fountain in the town center. One representative of each family on eRada was there each day to give thanks.

The truffles served as barter for goods required to sustain eRada's population. After the offering each member slowly crushed one plump truffle in their mouth, where the taste oozed into a caramel-like liquid gold as it slipped down the palate. Liquid gold releasing the exact DNA of that virtue into every cell of the family member. Because the offering and consumption occurs daily, each inhabitant on eRada was fully expressed with many, many virtues and with robust health.

I was hoping when we met again the next day, she would explain more about the unique topography ... and who lives on eRada.

The Narrator asks:
Do you think her new friend Van fits into the picture?
Who Inhabits eRada?
You were 'this close' to the mystery of the disc in this episode!

FIVE

The following day the girl took the same route home from work to the bus stop and found herself looking for her new friend Van, even before she got to the nursery.

Sure enough, she saw him watering shrubs right away. He smiled as she approached. He hadn't smiled like this when they met the day before. Oh! Her heart warmed as she saw inside his big warm smile, there was a narrow space between his two, straight front teeth.

She was late for the bus, so waved as she passed by, and said smiling back, asking, "See you tomorrow?"

She heard him call after her, still smiling, "You bet! Bring me some chocolate, will you?"

Episode Five — First Inhabitants

When eRada first formed, the order of business for the Gods was to determine …

- Who would be the first inhabitants?
- How many would there be?
- How would they be selected?
- On what basis would they be chosen?

All good questions as life on eRada was going to include more than green plants, water, earth, and sky.

eRada was so special. Its natural resources, enveloped in the DNA of various virtues, the inhabitant's character also had to match the level of specialness.

It was determined by the Gods that the first inhabitants would be Divine Spirits, each exemplifying the virtues outlined in the cypher they created to work from, below.

There would be twelve Divine Spirits; six male and six female, sent on a mission to populate and develop eRada. Each would have a primary virtue, a secondary virtue, and 'whisps' of a third, ancillary value.

This made them rich spirits that work well together and would populate the planet.

Virtues	Primary 1	Secondary	Ancillary Virtue
Male	Mercy	Forgiveness	Thankfulness
Male	Courage	Honor	Determination
Male	Honesty	Trust	Truth
Male	Service	Excellence	Reliability
Male	Tolerance	Humility	Caring
Male	Unity	Responsibility	Faithfulness
Female	Modesty	Kindness	Joyfulness
Female	Generosity	Love	Tact
Female	Compassion	Patience	Loyalty
Female	Justice	Respect	Detachment
Female	Enthusiasm	Creativity	Self Discipline
Female	Gentleness	Reverence	Peacefulness

One male and one female will join as lifetime mates as shown below.

Male offspring are born with the primary virtue of the male parent and the female offspring are born with the primary virtue of the female parent. They also received a sprinkling of each parent's secondary and ancillary virtues.

This way the population will be a healthy cross section of virtuous souls who share private and community tasks on eRada.

- Unity and Generosity parents yield an offspring with both virtues.
- Mercy and Modesty parents yield an offspring with both virtues.
- Honesty and Enthusiasm parents yield an offspring with both virtues.
- Service and Gentleness parents yield an offspring with both virtues.
- Courage and Justice parents yield an offspring with both virtues.

Male	Male	Male	Male	Male	Male
Unity	Mercy	Service	Honesty	Courage	Tolerance

eRada Lineage

Generosity	Modesty	Gentleness	Enthusiasm	Justice	Compassion
Female	Female	Female	Female	Female	Female

The Narrator:

In a coming episode, you will meet the offspring of two Divine Spirits, who become emissaries from eRada to our planet, Earth, bringing these magical truffles as gifts to our world.

You will also witness the role of the 'Old Souls' sent to teach the males the wisdom of life.

And you will see the unusual method of transport of males around eRada!

Hang on from more on the disc ...

SIX

I didn't' see the girl for the next few days as I was teaching during her work breaks when we could meet. I kept looking at the map I drew and finding more and more questions for which I wanted answers.

The next day the girl skipped her work break so she could slip out early and stop at the nursery before catching the bus home. She was going to see Van again. She felt herself actually skipping as she left the chocolate shoppe.

Each day that week she brought him a truffle to sample from that day's batch. What she didn't know (and never would) was that Van was just as excited to see her at the end of his day as she was to see him. [I bet she would have loved to know that.]

There he stood among the lush and fragrant small cedar trees in the nursery, flashing his broad, toothy smile. "Why did she find the gap between his two front teeth endearing," she thought to herself? She could not remember ever meeting anyone that had the same kind of gap, except a boy in her class in middle school who had it corrected with braces.

Walking toward him that day felt magical, which she shared with me … 'why magical' at a later meeting. His grey-green eyes sparkled, and she could see the copper and gold flecks in his eyes, and the soft and thick, bronze lashes framing them.

By the third day that week as she made her way the nursery, she literally felt like she was 'gliding' toward his now outstretch arms. Enfolded in his brief embrace she noticed she felt a warm glow as she stepped back, and they began talking. It was amazing she told me how much they could talk about in fifteen minutes.

"What's the flavor today," he asked on that third day.

"Raspberry! I almost forgot!" she said as she reached in the vest pocket of her Pendleton. She nearly forgot to grab one, remembered, and dropped the sample in her pocket as she walked out the door.

As her fingertips felt the slippery chocolate shell, she felt something else in her pocket, underneath the chocolate. Oh, yes, she remembered. The disc! The last time she touched it was after her shower several days before.

Fifteen minutes later he watched her turn and head out of the nursery and down the sidewalk toward her bus stop.

He found her captivating and beautiful. Their conversations were light yet everything she said ... every word she spoke ... felt intense to him. Every word was important to hear and absorb. He didn't want to miss anything.

Today was the first time he finally opened his arms up to her as she approached, and it felt wonderful! It was not sexual ... he knew that feeling for sure. This was different.

"How kind she is," he thought, "to bring me truffle samples and listen attentively as I pontificate the pleasures of taking the truffle whole into my mouth, sucking it a few times to release the outer chocolate goodness, then closing my mouth, allowing my gums (not teeth) to crush it, releasing the raspberry flavor in a gush, then sliding down my throat."

"She listened to me," he thought. As Van thought back over his last two relationships, he couldn't ever remember a girlfriend listening to him this closely and kindly.

As he fell asleep that night, her face was the last image on the screen of his mind.

As the girl fell asleep that night, it was his face she saw as the last image on the screen of her mind.

Episode SIX — Life on eRada

The girl entered her dream almost immediately.

Life on eRada included the upper, middle, and ground elevations ... and below ground of this oddly shaped planet, with three suns and four hours of night based on its odd climate.

The Divine Spirits and their families live in the upper elevations, where truffles are harvested daily and grow in winding moss beds around the mountains. (Graphic renderings of eRada shown in Episodes 3 and 4.)

The female Divine Spirits are blessed with a placket of skin along their middle spine which can open, under specific circumstances, revealing a large set of wings. It is not unusual to see a female transporting her male partner across the lands to study with the Old Souls.

The Divine Souls, better known as the 'Old Souls' live in middle elevations, in the caverns that run near the surface of the planet. Old Souls have undergone a spiritual transformation into another form and are where the male Divine Spirits study and learn about the world of spirituality and virtues. It is also not unusual to see a female after transporting her male partner by wing, at the knee of her male, as he has long spiritual conversations that often exceed the four hours of night.

The Possibility of eRada

Below ground is where the truffle harvesting occurs every day. The temperature is cool and dry there; the perfect setting for keeping the truffles fresh for packaging and transport. With three suns and only four hours of night, when left unharvested, the truffles melted back into the soil within five days of blooming.

The ground elevations were made up of small lakes, rivers, streams, and plenty of wildlife. Water, however, is not like the water the girl, or you and I know it. It looks like water from a distance. Yet, as the girl hovered over the river and getting closer, she saw that it wasn't water at all in the river! The river and all water beds were filled with zillions of clear glass discs that were constantly flowing, like water.

There were the discs!

A lucid dreamer, she realized in her dream that she had a disc that came from eRada!!!

The Narrator asks:

How did a disc end up on the path to her mother's cottage?

How did inhabitants get water, if all there was in the rivers, streams and lakes were flowing discs?

How did the discs move continuously as though they were water?

These are questions to be answered in the next and upcoming Episodes.

SEVEN

The next morning, the girl dressed hurriedly and couldn't wait to get to work. She meant to stop at her mother's, but that was out now. Maybe after work she thought.

It was Monday and she spent two days exploring the City. Saturday was for the Zoo, at 42nd and Sloat and a few blocks from the beach. Her absolute favorite weekend adventures. Sometimes she would walk to the beach after doing the whole zoo. It was about six blocks away.

When she chose a day at the beach instead of the Zoo, she would hike to Fort Funston, an old fort on the beach used by the military to protect the coast. She would walk through the windy concrete, domed tunnels and come out to stand on the beach imagining what it must have been like during wartime.

On Sunday, she gathered leaves and buds around the old Victorian and made a large centerpiece for her table in the foyer. Not many people visited the girl. Deliveries were made around the back near the kitchen. She loved coming in the front door every day and being greeted by her very own seasonal creation.

She wore her favorite Pendleton and all the way across the Golden Gate, she turned the disc, still in her pocket, over and over in her fingers. Right before she was to reach up and pull the bell for her stop, the girl squeezed her nostrils together with her fingers (like she inhaled pepper) and when she did, she quickly took an involuntary, sharp breath in through her nose, and saw stars again,' and then coughed twice.

"Wait," she hollered to the bus driver, and she dropped the disc in her pocket, grabbed her purse, and rushed to the front of the bus. The bus took a big lurch forward as it stopped short. She righted herself, smiled at the driver and said, "thank you," and stepped off the two big steps onto Market Street, a few blocks from the chocolate shoppe.

The shoppe was well known in San Francisco for having handmade organic truffles, fresh every day. The J&S handmade chocolates metal sign hung over the entry; the truffles were beautifully crafted one by one, with the finest Belgian chocolate (Belcolade) and the most expensive extracts. The owner said often "our customers deserve the very best," particularly the week the invoices arrived for chocolate and essences.

All day the girl thought about Van as she rolled one hundred and twenty-five key lime truffles dipped in cocoa dust and packaged in boxes of five. They are beautiful she thought as she attached to each box an ingredient and product label, a logo label, a small bow and sealed it with a J&S decal. They were particularly fragrant today and it seemed to her that the dark chocolate truffles looked like glass. She snitched one and remembered thinking that these never tasted this good before. Key lime was her new favorite.

As fast as she could box these truffles, they seemed to fly off the shelves. It was Monday and they were very busy right before she left that day.

She slipped out the door forgetting the sample for Van and arrived at the nursery, already using up five of the fifteen minutes she had to visit.

When she arrived at the nursery that day after work, she didn't see him anywhere.

She quickly walked around the plants and shrubs and then hurried to the small business office in the back.

The owner of the nursery was running numbers on an old adding machine when she walked in. It jammed after pressing almost every key, so he stopped every few seconds, adjusted the keys, grumbled, and continued, repeating the pattern.

He was engrossed in this task so he didn't hear her come in, over the tapping and straightening the machine keys.

She watched for a minute or two and then interrupted, "excuse me, sir" she said as he looked up at her. "I'm looking for Van. Do you know where he is?"

The man looked at her, paused and then stood up, stretching his legs, then lifting his arms above his head, cracking his knuckles. Then he asked, "Come again? Who?"

"Van!! The student intern working here from the university!." she said, trying not to sound too irritated because he took so long to answer her to begin with, and that she only had a few minutes left to catch the bus. "He's studying agriculture there."

"There's no Van working here," the owner said and turned back around, sat down and began running numbers again.

Before he got to the third key, which stalled, she asked, exasperated by now, "you mean he did work here and now he's gone?"

The owner slowly turned back around, looked at her, paused and said, without getting up this time, "Look, I don't know what you are talking about young lady. I have never had an intern here from the university and the only helper I have is my granddaughter when she is on break from school, and she's sixteen."

"But that's just not possible," she thought she said to herself, but likely not to say it out loud, as he shook his head, went back to work, as she hurriedly walked out of the office, back through the nursery, having one more good look for him, and out of the shop and on to the bus stop.

As she ran bleary-eyed now to the sidewalk outside the nursery, the fragrance of the cedar trees hit her in the face and literally stopped her in her tracks. She sneezed, and then ran all the way to the bus stop.

Lee cried on the ride home ... that's her name, by the way ... Lee.

Her tears were heavy and salty, and she wasn't even sure why she was crying. She thought ... I'm melting like the disc. She had been rolling it around between her fingers in her pocket again as she heard the bus bells and felt each stop and start along the way home.

Lee fell asleep that night, tears on her pillow, asking out loud, "Van, where did you go? Were you even there? Were you a dream? Am I crazy ... because I know I felt your arms around me."

Episode Seven — Sustaining Life

The Girl entered her dream almost immediately that night.

She was right back, hovering over the river, and saw that the 'water' in the river wasn't water at all! The river and waterways were filled with zillions of clear glass discs, three inches in diameter, that were constantly flowing, like water!

The generous and spiritual nature of all those living on eRada was an integral part of their lives.

When a female offspring was betrothed to another, they are gifted their own family

Urn of Life following the ceremony. The Urn is how everyone lived!

Once each day every married female walks the same path at the same time to the town square and the stone fountain where discs are flowing constantly. When scooped into the Urn of Life, the discs instantly liquify after a prayer, and that is the daily water for the family. Of course, if more is needed it is often that the female will make a second trip to the fountain … and even a third. There is no shortage of these discs.

While gathering her daily supply of water, each female speaks a prayer to thank their parents and the original twelve spirits that first were chosen to inhabit eRada. At the fountain you can hear numerous female voices dipping, praying and whispering this prayer repeatedly, all while getting their daily sustenance of 'water.'

Hail to the Spirits that guide us, day in and day out,
We offer our gratitude and ever-present love,
For your protection of our peace and harmony,
Knowing you are watching us from above.
Our greatest good is what we wish for one another,
The gift you give to every father, child, and mother.
Behold the miracle of eRada, your gift to us,
To live where all are one, Hail to the Spirits that guide us.

The continual chanting by the females at the fountain, giving thanks, created a melodic harmony, like a cluster of butterflies gliding in the breeze. The words as they were spoken produced tufts of tiny bubbles, which rose from their mouths, up and into the atmosphere. In her dream the girl squinted at the myriad of bubbles rising from around the fountain ... why they looked like stars she thought. Remember she has lucid dreams so she can think while dreaming.

As the girl got closer to the fountain in the city square, she saw the discs moving like water again, and very shortly, she saw something unusual. Those discs were forced and sourced by a furious wind from tunnels beneath the surface of eRada that feed into every waterway and find their exit into the atmosphere.

The Narrator:

Episode 8 will reveal the mystery of how that one disc ended up on the path to Lee's mother's cottage.

Meet the offspring of two Spirit partners who won the honor of being the Emissaries from eRada to the world.

Leslie Thomas Flowers

EIGHT

She awoke that morning to sunlight streaming in through the stained-glass window in her bedroom. The turret was round, and the windows were small, decorated with gardenias, the girl's favorite, as is her mother's. Somehow, she thought she got a light whiff of gardenia when she focused her gaze on the blooms in the window.

Today the girl was going to finally talk to her mother about the disc she found ... and how she met Van not long ago and how he disappeared. Her mother would likely have ideas about this. In any event she needed someone to talk to.

Right now, she spent so much time at work ... and she had no interest in talking about her life with the owner of Janeslee & Sylvain Handmade Chocolates.

She grabbed her purse, a sandwich for lunch, and her Pendleton, and bounded down the back stairs, heading to her mother's cottage. The sun had been breaking through the fog, which didn't happen at 8:00 am typically and it shed dancing light along the pine needle path. She loved living here in such a beautiful place and close to her mother.

As the door to the cottage opened, the waft of fresh coffee filled the air ... mother smiled, hugged the girl and invited her to have a seat at the small kitchen table, which overlooked her mother's garden, filled of course with the last blooms of her gardenias for the season.

Oooh, mother had made fresh biscuits this morning, riddled with sharp cheddar cheese. She knew her daughter loved these. Coffee poured, cream added, biscuits buttered, and mother sat down at the table.

"Mother," the girl said, "I've been wanting to show you something." She reached in her pocket, took out the disc, and laid it on the table by her mother's coffee cup.

"I found this on the path coming here about a week ago after a rainstorm. Do you know what it is?"

Her mother touched the disc ever so lightly with her forefinger, then looked up at her daughter thoughtfully, as though she was getting ready to say something. She paused.

"What?" the girl asked impatiently. "What?"

"Do you know what it is mother? When I touch it, my fingers are wet, and something so strange happened. When I first found the disc, I sneezed and by the time I got to your porch, the flowers appeared to explode in color."

"What is it? How did it get here?" She kept firing questions at her mother, one after the other.

"That," said her mother, "is a 'disc of life'."

"Huh?" she said. "A what?"

Her mother smiled and leaned back in the ladder-back chair that had been in their family since she was a little girl, now rubbed with age where the chair back met the table edge, looked up and said with another smile and a wink, and said, "watch this."

As her mother began to whisper these words aloud, almost like a song, she took the girl's forefinger and her own and placed both tips directly on the disc.

Hail to the Spirits that guide us, day in and day out,
We offer our gratitude and ever-present love,
For your protection of our peace and harmony,
Knowing you are watching us from above.
Our greatest good is what we wish for one another,
The gift you give to every father, child, and mother.
Behold the miracle of eRada, your gift to us,
To live where all are one, Hail to the Spirits that guide us.

Before her mother had finished, the disc melted on the table … and … was gone, leaving a small pool of water.

Episode Eight — The Emissaries

Once truffle harvesting was in full swing on eRada, which included a lot of hard work setting up the underground processing and packaging for distributing the magic truffles through the galaxy, it was time to select the first emissaries from eRada. The emissaries were one male and one female with an extraordinary propensity toward consistently living their virtues.

Many offspring of the original spirits now had their own children, and all the children of that generation considered it to be an honor to be selected emissaries to the world. All good deeds done by offspring were recorded in the family journal and these acts were part of the process of selecting the emissaries from eRada to bring their magic truffles to the world.

In fact, for the first judging, both Freya and Odin from the old Norse god collective were invited to participate in the judging. These Norse gods had much experience in determining the highest quality of value in their own countrymen.

And so it was that a daughter of mother's Generosity and father's Unity, and a son of mother Justice and father Courage were selected. They came from a long line of highly visible and generous spirits and were well known by fellow eRadans.

These two met as did all the children, when they were toddlers in a nursery commune, where they were carefully watched over during the harvesting and manufacturing and distribution days, deep within the planet.

Each day an 'old soul' would travel to the commune and teach the children the history of eRada, the origin of their values, spirituality, geography (in case they became emissaries), and about the values of all the gods of the world. They spent their days listening, playing games, laughing, and

The Possibility of eRada

napping at the knee of the old soul. Life was free and easy for them, just as life was in most cases for inhabitants of eRada.

All the children on eRada were like brothers and sisters, each exemplifying the virtue of their parents, and of course their grandparents before them. Each generation of eRadans became more focused on exhibiting and sharing their virtues through their deeds.

The emissaries managed the world distribution of the magic truffles, returning home each year with supplies and tools from other worlds, that rounded out life on eRada. They came back with foods, spices, and herbs … and stories told to the children in faraway places.

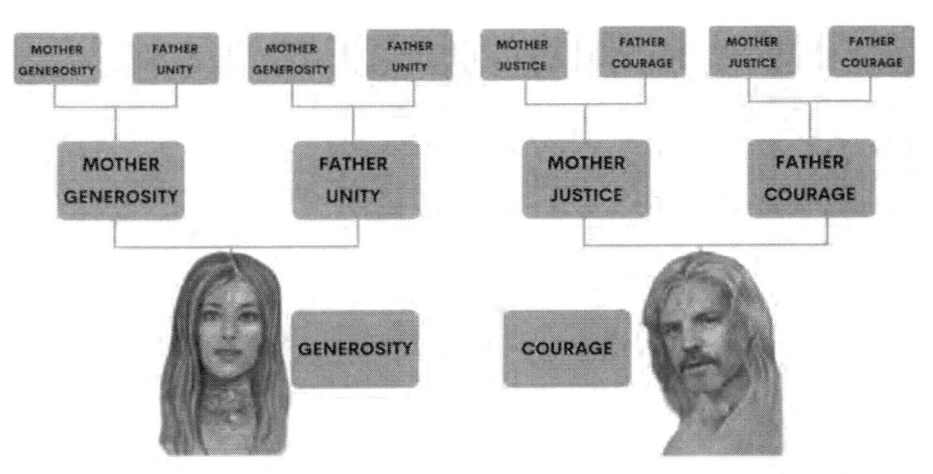

MOTHER GENEROSITY	FATHER UNITY	MOTHER GENEROSITY	FATHER UNITY	MOTHER JUSTICE	FATHER COURAGE	MOTHER JUSTICE	FATHER COURAGE
MOTHER GENEROSITY		FATHER UNITY		MOTHER JUSTICE		FATHER COURAGE	
	GENEROSITY				COURAGE		

While not mentioned before, there exists a negative force within eRada which will be revealed in a later episode. You will learn of the Spirit Demons, who constantly hover and flit over and around the mountains, sucking up the tender plant life that keeps eRada in environmental balance, also small wildlife, and the precious truffles when the wildlife wasn't enough to appease their hunger.

They seemed to prefer the truffles filled with blueberry, although they also made a huge dent in the raspberry ones. Packaging results revealed this daily 'loss' of those truffles. Spirit Demons travel the planet via the intertwining wind tunnels, that forced the course of discs in the water beds.

Narrator:

Episode 9 will begin to reveal the lineage of the girl and her mother.

You will learn the Story of the selected female emissary.

NINE

Before her mother had finished, the disc melted on the table … and … was gone, leaving only a small, flat pool of water …

The girl was flabbergasted! Her mother did this?

Perhaps she was no different than most grown children. She never really paid much attention to what her mother was doing all the years of her childhood, then at school, then off to work. Before they moved to Marin County, her father worked at the Green Shoe Factory in Boston where Stride Rite shoes were manufactured, ran the stitching department, drove an hour into work and home … she didn't really know him either.

"Mother, what is going on here," she said with a twinkle in her eye and a half smile.

Her mother began this way …

When I was a little girl, I never knew my grandparents. My mother told me stories about them and that they were descendants of the Northmen, also known as Vikings. They settled in Kiev Russia where they raised their families.

Grandfather was a Knight and Grandmother was an Earl and they met for the first time on their wedding day. Betrothed at age eleven, they communicated by messenger over the years. Many messages were lost; some showing up years after being sent. It was amazing how their love persisted for decades.

Her mother stopped and said, "wait a minute…"

She got up and climbed up a pull-down staircase into the small attic, above the kitchen. The girl poured herself another cup of coffee. She wondered why her mother hadn't ever talked about her grandparents before. She was also kicking herself for not paying more attention to her parents. Looks like mother had a magical and mysterious life.

"Found it," she heard her mother's holler float right down and through the wood ceiling. There, in the corner of the attic, covered with dust was a small trunk with splintering wood spines, dried with age, and a leather handle. It was thick with dust where the blanket covering it had slipped halfway off at some point long ago.

"Found it," she heard her mother's holler float right down and through the wood ceiling. There, in the corner of the attic, covered with dust was a small trunk with splintering wood spines, dried with age, and a leather handle. It was thick with dust where the blanket covering it had slipped halfway off at some point long ago.

Opening it, her mother reached in and carefully fingered past several thinning layers of aging raw silk, to reveal a crown. Simple, tarnished, yet it had survived time ... over twelve hundred years and was last worn by Lee's great grandmother when she met her betrothed. As an Earl, she was granted the rights in Kiev as a landowner and therefore a queen-of-sorts. This was her crown!

Lee's mother began to cry as she realized this ancient relic had been buried in her attic without a care for the whole of the girl's life and was never shared. "Water under the bridge," the mother was fond of saying. I'll make it right, right now. Now is all we have, after all.

She gently lifted the crown from underneath all the layers of silk and carried it gently, like a newborn baby, down the attic stairs, step by step and walked to the table. Cradling the small package in one arm, she moved the coffee cups, biscuit plate, and utensils to the side with one hand, then gently lowered the silks onto the table.

"Lee," her mother said, "Let me tell you a story about my grandparents."

Episode Nine — Everyday Life on eRada

eRada's Female emissary, Jaya-Li (Jaya for short), was the daughter of her mother's generosity and her father's sense of unity. She lived with her brother and parents near the upper crust of eRada. Their home was built into a hill where the beds of magic truffles served as their roof and maintained a gentle coolness within. With four hours of night and three suns, it was the perfect scenario for inhabitants.

The openings to the outside of the hill were three small windows and a door. Other than those four places a passerby would never realize there was a home there if they didn't notice the openings.

Inside in the far-right corner as one enters, sits a very large white stone fireplace, with an opening for wood log storage. The fireplace was six feet in diameter with a wrought iron arm from one side to the other for hanging pots of stock, broth, and hot water for cooking, and to keep the main room warm.

Next to the fireplace in the back of the room was a small pantry and next to that was an open cabinet where the family dishes were kept. Across from the fireplace was a single bed offered to the occasional traveler, and there is a narrow staircase leading to an upstairs, further inside the hill. The upstairs had one large room with two large beds where the family slept.

A table and four chairs sat in the center of the large room with two ladder backed chairs, handmade by Jaya's father, and a small woven rug. The floor was laid with wide, long planks of cedar, which grew naturally on eRada and had their home always fragrant with cedar and warm smoke, as it was absorbed into the wood.

Her mother had a modest garden about fifty feet away from the house, filled with flowers, fruits and vegetables that adored and thrived under long, long days of warm sun. She cultivated year-round oranges and a berry something like a strawberry as the girl knew it, along with corn, spinach, and tomatoes.

Hunting for game on eRada was restricted and organized to give each family ample food all year round. There are vast forests in addition to the truffle beds, and the environmental balance was overseen by eRada's chosen male emissary, Stuvan. [You'll meet Stuvan in another episode.]

Jaya's brother, Aadi, was half her age when a great turbulence occurred within the center of eRada, causing critical weather implications. The livelihood of eRada depended on the consistent nature of their climate. Any disturbance could affect the crops and thereby their livelihood. And above all, the distribution of magic truffles in every corner of the known world, which was their primary focus.

A disturbance happened one late afternoon when Jaya had finished her work for the day. That included going with mother to the fountain for their daily spiritual walk, prayer, and retrieval of 'water,' tending to mother's garden, several hours within eRada, schoolwork with the master, and working in packaging or sorting magic truffles underground.

She often wandered along her favorite stream, laid down and cuddled into the thick and lush green moss that grew along both sides of the stream … and napped.

While sleeping, a storm began, blowing monstrous winds from within the planet, through the tunnels, and to the surface. The winds were so strong that Jaya rolled down the small mossy hill and right into the stream and was quickly swept away by the now rushing discs. She knew she could not reach the shore while being pushed downstream at this rate, so she lay back and did the only thing she could do … ride it until it ended. For surely it would end, she thought. Surely it would end.

Narrator:

Episode 10 will reveal the mystery of the crown, more on how that one disc ended up on the path to Lee's mother's cottage.

What happens during Jaya's furious ride down the blowing aqua discs in the stream?

TEN

After gently setting the crown on the table, "Lee," her mother said, "Let me tell you a story about my grandparents."

"Wait," the girl asked … "before you do, how is it you've had this crown and I never knew? And what about that disc and that prayer, mother?"

Her mother poured herself another coffee and took a bite of a biscuit and began to talk. "I almost forgot about that crown," she said. "Isn't that odd."

"They say that when my grandfather first met and kissed his bride, her crown slipped off her head and onto her breast between them." She went on sharing the old story and told the girl that he laughed, placed her crown back on her head, and kissed her again!

When grandfather went off to war, grandmother gave him the crown for luck, which he tucked at the bottom of his arrow pouch, always with him in battle. And when he came home, he placed the crown back on her head as a ritual. This was his good luck charm as he lived to the ripe old age of fifty and survived many wars.

Episode Ten — An Incredible Journey

Jaya-Li closed her eyes, tucked her hands under her hips and fell into a light nap-sleep as she was catapulted down the river, riding on the discs, rushing furiously.

When she was little, there were minor disturbances like this, forced by the Spirit Demons who, it seemed, lived only to disrupt the delicate nature and environment on eRada. Her father and other children's fathers, crafted 'rafts' of large caladium leaves, held together with wiry twigs from the birch trees that grew in dotted stands around the planet. If you squinted your eyes as you traveled above the trees to go to school or to study, males on the backs of the females, it looked like the trees were puffs of clouds or snow dotting the landscape.

As Jaya was swiftly catapulted down the riverbed, overhead she watched one of the females transporting a basket of the magic truffles from the surface of eRada to manufacturing and packaging, and then circled back to retrieve another.

While females transport males, they also use their wings to quickly pluck the tender truffles from their beds and move them into the dark and cool underground to preserve their shine and intensity of flavor, and their 'magic.'

This is Freya, pictured, named by her parents after a Viking god they both knew very well before they were selected to inhabit and populate eRada.

The ride down the riverbed could last several days before the storm subsided. It depended on how angry the Spirit Demons were and how fast Stuvan could gain environmental control again on eRada. [You'll meet Stuvan in Episode 11.]

As the hours went by and she moved down river, Jaya kept seeing the image of a person, a man, walking along the shore. How could they keep up? She didn't know how fast she was going, yet there he was!

[The girl turned over and sat straight up in bed in the middle of the night! The image she was sure was Van! How could that be she wondered, flopped back down, turned on her side, and went back into her dream.]

Finally, after three days of turbulence, the winds subsided, and she walked, wobbly legged to the shore. Now for the long walk back to her home. Oh, she was so hungry and could almost smell the rabbit stew mother always seemed to have simmering over the hearth.

The Narrator:

Episode 11 reveals Where is Van?

The girl needles her mother for more information about her past.

ELEVEN

It was a week or so before I was able to meet with Lee again. I met her at the coffee shop over her lunch hour. I couldn't wait to find out if anything was new since we last met …. probably not. I was interested in seeing if she was still having that dream.

I got there first and took a seat at the window looking out on the dead-end alley, just off a busy street between Chinatown and Nob-Hill. The alley was narrow and on one side was a long, blank warehouse wall with minimal redesign. Now there were several dwellings there, each with entry into the alley and with a window.

At the end of the alley was a tall narrow building of flats, where five escape ladders built a stairway to the sky. Behind each ladder, there were identical windows … a big one in the middle and two smaller ones on either side.

As I waited for Lee, I saw several children squatting on the curb across the way, making signs out of cardboard box flaps. Two got up and began batting a racquetball against the door of one home. The door opened and they were greeted by a lurching and barking old German Shepherd, followed by a woman who pulled the dog back in by the collar, smiled at the children, and closed the door.

In bounded Lee wearing a Pendleton over her full-frontal apron, covered with chocolate and some green and pink food coloring of some sort. I smelled raspberries!

"Do I smell raspberry," I asked her. She laughed shaking her head and pretending to wipe her apron and lick her fingers smiling. "My favorite," she said.

"So …has anything happened since we met last week?" I wanted to hear more about her dream.

Before I knew it Lee began talking about Van, who she met the week before at the nursery on the way home, and how he disappeared! She described him as tall, with copper hair and a small separation between his two front teeth. She talked about their simple hugs that felt so comforting and warm. And then she began to cry.

"What do you mean, he disappeared," I asked. "And why are you crying? You only knew him briefly, right?"

"After two brief visits on my way home, one day when I went by the nursery, and I couldn't find him anywhere! When I found the owner and asked him about it, he insisted no one named Van worked there!"

"Do you think it's possible that I never met him? And this was part of those very strange dreams," she asked.

Episode Eleven — Meet Stuvan

[From Episode Ten] Finally, after three days of turbulence, the winds subsided, and Jaya walked, wobbly legged to the shore. Now for the long walk back to her home. Oh, she was so hungry and could almost smell the rabbit stew mother always seemed to have simmering over the hearth.

You may be wondering Why Jaya-Li didn't simple 'release and open her wings' to get home, rather than walk. The use of wings is restricted to first, any emergency that required fast transport of truffles to production, and second, transporting the males to the knee of the Old Souls where they study every day.

eRada's male emissary is Stuvan who grew up with Jaya-Li and is the son of his mother's courage and his father's unity. His father had been managing the delicate environmental balance on eRada since its inception. Stuvan now has this role and protects the forests and all living things on the planet, along with the truffles, the harvesting, planting, and maintenance.

Stuvan's biggest challenge was the Spirit Demons who constantly hovered over the mountain, sucking up plants, creatures, and truffles, when they were hungry. They were always hungry.

As a youth, Stuvan developed a solution to the hungry Spirit Demons. His system provided consistent nourishment for them so that the mountain range ecology remained pristine.

Each day he gathered up the bits of trees and flowers that were naturally sluffed off and placed them in a great pile of offerings in the center of a large meadow. As the Spirit Demons were attracted to fire, Stuvan would create a small narrow lane around the pile of nourishment and set it on fire. The fire self-extinguished swiftly, yet not until after the Spirit Demons made a beeline to the feast. Much more efficient than foraging.

Unfortunately for managing the ecosystem on eRada, Spirit Demons and Old Souls (teachers) had altercations frequently. They both use the wind tunnels that fuel the water beds to reach the surface of eRada.

It took all of Stuvan's mental prowess to manage the Spirit Demons and the Old Souls, in addition to his environmental responsibilities on eRada.

He has his own Spiritual Guide of sorts in Lalla. Many creatures live on eRada, but none to compare with what we might call a bear, whose telepathic powers are greater than any spirits on eRada.

Stuvan's parents presented him with the dark brown, thick-coated, fat bellied cub Lalla on his 2nd birthday and now, at approximately 16 earth years, Lalla remains Stuvan's closest friend and ally.

As Stuvan grew and learned how to protect the forests at his father's side, Lalla offered great insights into preserving ecological and planet balance so that the finest truffles would spring up through the heavy moss beds that covered the forest and mountain beds, and peace would be enjoyed among all spirits.

Lalla can foresee what might happen when certain solutions are required to manage the environment or a skirmish between the 'souls,' and image them in real time for Stuvan to follow. At these fortuitous moments, Lalla will lie face down on the moss and in between truffle beds, with legs and arms splayed, and hum a certain group of notes, three times in a row.

Then, just above the Lalla, appears a hologram of events playing out like our newsreels. He might offer several solutions in a few minutes, depending on the challenge. Stuvan would then study them and choose which avenue to follow based on these visions. Lalla served as a second sight or additional layer of intuition for Stuvan.

Lalla is five feet tall on all fours, his paws have two extra digits at each heel, allowing him to gather great speed in his lumbering trot. When running at full clip, it took Stuvan from boyhood into manhood to keep stride with his beloved Lalla.

While growing up, these two spent countless hours frolicking in the waterbeds on the mountain, sun shining in their faces, both spirit and guide were like siblings.

When harvesting season was over, they would stuff themselves with the truffles that grew around the very edges of the field. These edges were left for those who required more of their passion and spirituality and succulent flavor. The spirits had heard about this effort when former emissaries came to earth and stumbled on the most popular book on that planet, what they call the New Testament.

The Narrator:

In Episode 12 The girl needles her mother for more information about her past.

Twelve

It was late when Lee got home that night; it had been a long day at work. She took out a burrito from the freezer and nuked it, poured a large glass of water, and headed upstairs.

The moon in her bedroom cast a bright light, flooding through the stained-glass window, casting magical shadows from tree limbs, gently waving in the night breeze.

She undressed and sat mindlessly eating her burrito, looking out the window onto the rolling landscape and could see the roof of her mother's cottage from there.

After dinner, she crawled into bed, never noticing that the crown mother had shown her yesterday, sat on a chair in a dark corner of her room.

Snuggled in, she smiled and welcomed sleep, which came right away.

Then she thought she felt something touching her head … she knew she was asleep. Then she felt a strong arm, wrapping around her waist, as she was lifted out of her bed.

She woke with a start! Van was standing in her bedroom! It was his arm wrapped around her waist!

He adjusted the crown he had placed on her head, pulled her even tighter, kissed her full lips hungrily and deeply, and said, "Hold on, I've got something to show you."

"What? Wait," she said, still flushed from the rush of his kiss! "How are you here? Where have you been?" She had so many questions.

Van lifted her into his arms, touched her crown, and they both floated eerily up and through the turret roof as though it wasn't there, and out into the moonlit night sky.

Episode Twelve — Arrival

It was night on eRada when Van and Lee floated from the dark sky down into the atmosphere of eRada and landed gently in the middle of a wild truffle bed.

"Where are we?" Lee asked, feeling a little dizzy.

He said, "We are home, Lee."

When she looked up at him, she was in shock! He did not look like 'her Van,' the Van she met at the nursery … not exactly. It was him … but he looked middle aged now! "Oh my God," she thought to herself. "What's going on here?"

Van laughed when he saw the look on her face. "Lee," he said, "you look older too! And so beautiful."

She felt her face with her fingertips, then around her eyes and her mouth. It was different; older, sagging?

"Where are we," she asked him again.

"We are home, Lee," he said.

It had taken forty years of travel, he explained, from the moment we left your bedroom in San Francisco to arrive here, on eRada. While it felt to Lee like it was a few moments, she had lost all sense of time.

"I want you to meet two very special people tomorrow," he told her. "They are our younger selves."

"Huh? This is all too much, Van. You mean there are two versions of us," she asked.

"Yes. We are forty years older than they are! So, we get to see and get to know our younger selves!"

"Tomorrow," he said, "You will meet Jaya-Li and Stuvan; you and me." He smiled, looking down into her eyes and brushed her cheek with the back of his hand.

It was night and the three moons were shining brightly over eRada during its daily, four-hour stretch.

Van adjusted her crown again, pulled her very close, and kissed her gently for a long, long time. With arms wrapped tightly around one another, gazing up at the moon, they nestled down into the soft truffle bed and both fell into a deep sleep.

As they slept, dreaming about tomorrow, the dreams were warm and filled with night sounds, seeming to emanate all around them.

THIS ENDS PART I

To view the seven-minute book trailer go to *YouTube*.

About the Author

Already an acclaimed writer, in her new book, Leslie Flowers invites you to explore what could be! With a passion for exploring the human condition and the mysteries of the universe, this book blends together values, virtues and soul kissing love ... a place we remember and love.

In her career, Leslie has demonstrated remarka-ble versatility, adaptability, and resilience in inspiring and motivating aspiring and emerging leaders to excel in their lives and professions. Her lifelong passion for learning kickstarted an intellectual and emotional journey that has taken her through corporate publishing, entrepreneurship, board service, women's empowerment, and immersion into professional development, focusing on human performance and achievement.

Leslie Flowers differentiates as an advisor and educator through her speaking, mastermind facilitation, broadcasting, writing, and instructional design, in which she integrates Dr. Napoleon Hill's foundational treatise on personal improvement, "Think and Grow Rich." She is the architect of "The 12 Laws of Achievement," a proven, repeatable success framework for unlocking leadership
-

potential, increasing self awareness, and driving extraordinary results through goal setting, visualization, and collaboration.

Insights and Discoveries

The Possibility of eKada

In each episode of this story there are things to ponder.

You may have an insight, a memory, or even a light bulb moment when reading.

These next pages are for you to date and jot down these moments of reflection to review, repeat, and perhaps one day look back at how far you've come in developing a strong sense of character and confidence.

Enjoy, Leslie Flowers

CREDITS

Some artworks by Ian Daniels art purchased rights March 2004 via Duirwaigh gallery.

Some graphics purchased by artists on Fiverr.

Logo designed by Flaxenfield Design Studio Chapel Hill NC USA.